MONSTERS
AN IMAGINATION LIBRARY SERIES

Monsters of the Deep

by Janet Perry and Victor Gentle

*To Matthew Wechter, who swims and sings and
leaps in the water better than any mermaid*

Gareth Stevens Publishing
MILWAUKEE

For a free color catalog describing Gareth Stevens' list of high-quality books and multimedia programs, call 1-800-542-2595 (USA) or 1-800-461-9120 (Canada). Gareth Stevens Publishing's Fax: (414) 225-0377.

Library of Congress Cataloging-in-Publication Data

Perry, Janet, 1960-
  Monsters of the deep / by Janet Perry and Victor Gentle.
    p. cm. — (Monsters: an imagination library series)
  Includes bibliographical references (p. 22) and index.
  Summary: Discusses some of the large and frightening creatures that live, or are believed to have lived, in the world's oceans.
  ISBN 0-8368-2440-7 (lib. bdg.)
  1. Marine animals—Juvenile literature. 2. Sea monsters—Juvenile literature. [1. Marine animals. 2. Sea monsters.] I. Gentle, Victor. II. Title. III. Series: Perry, Janet, 1960- Monsters.
  QL122.2.P45 1999
  578.77—dc21   99-22864

First published in 1999 by
Gareth Stevens Publishing
1555 North RiverCenter Drive, Suite 201
Milwaukee, WI 53212 USA

Text: Janet Perry and Victor Gentle
Page layout: Janet Perry, Victor Gentle, and Helene Feider
Cover design: Joel Bucaro and Helene Feider
Series editor: Patricia Lantier-Sampon
Editorial assistant: Diane Laska

Photo credits: Cover, p. 7 © Archive Photos; p. 5 © Popperfoto/Archive Photos; p. 9 © 1984 Joyce R. Wilson/Photo Researchers, Inc.; p. 11 © 1998 Mark Erdmann; p. 13 From the American Geographical Society Collection, University of Wisconsin-Milwaukee Library; p. 15 Peabody Museum, Harvard University, Photograph by Hillel Burger, © 1990, President and Fellows of Harvard College; p. 17 © Bob Cranston/Innerspace Visions; p. 19 © Doug Perrine/Innerspace Visions; p. 21 © Photofest

Printed in the United States of America

1 2 3 4 5 6 7 8 9 03 02 01 00 99

TABLE OF CONTENTS

Words that appear in the glossary are printed in **boldface**
type the first time they occur in the text.

MONSTER CATCH

You're wading along the shore, capturing little fish with your hands. Something catches your eye. Slowly, it rises out of the brown ooze between the waves. It has scales, flippers, and teeth. It's not a fish or a turtle. It's swimming closer, and closer, and . . . it's looking *right at you.*

But wait! Gulls are diving at it. Those scales! They're just slimy leaves. And that's an old plastic grocery bag bubbling up around it. It's not a monster. It's just a log with a dead fish and someone's trash on it. Whew!

The most famous photo of Nessie, Scotland's Loch Ness Monster? Or is it the upper tail of a thresher shark, as one shark hunter believes?

FISH HISTORY

The Gill Man in the 1954 movie *Creature from the Black Lagoon* is a **prehistoric** beast that somehow survived **extinction**.

Scientists in the movie think the creature is an ancient relative of modern human beings. One scientist points out that there are many "living **fossils**," or kinds of animals that have not changed for millions of years.

Some true living fossils are **lungfish**, sharks, and **coelacanths**.

The Gill Man rises angrily from the depths of the black lagoon, disturbed by fossil hunters. Soon, he will disturb *them*. They came for bones. *He's alive!*

LIVING FOSSILS

Lungfish were alive 400 million years ago, even before dinosaurs roamed the land. Unlike other fish, lungfish breathe air like land animals. Some scientists think this shows an important link between fish and humans.

Sharks swam in the oceans 150 million years ago, and the first coelacanths lived 400 million years ago. People have never thought that sharks were extinct, but scientists used to think coelacanths had been extinct for 50 million years. They were wrong!

African lungfish have **gills** and can breathe in water, like other fish. They also have lungs, and can breathe in air, like other lungfish and land animals.

I'M HIDING, I'M HIDING! YOU CAN'T FIND ME!

Until 1938, fossils were the only record of coelacanths. Experts thought they were extinct.

Then, near the coast of South Africa, a fisherman caught a large, blue, unknown fish. It weighed over 125 pounds (57 kilograms) and was 5 feet (1.5 meters) long. He contacted Marjorie Courtenay-Latimer, who collected odd sea animals for her museum in East London, South Africa.

She, in turn, contacted Dr. J. L. B. Smith, an **ichthyologist**, who told her the "monster" was a coelacanth.

Are other monsters like these lurking in dark waters, waiting to surprise us?

A live coelacanth caught in July, 1998, in the sea off Sulawesi, Indonesia — part of a new population of coelacanths identified by Dr. Mark Erdmann.

THE PLACE CALLED "HERE BE MONSTERS"

The scientists in the *Creature* movie made money to pay for their searches by putting the Gill Man on display. In reality, many early explorers did a similar thing to make money.

Some early European maps have areas marked "Here Be Monsters." Sailors would go there to seek adventure or to find fortune. Many returned with strange creatures, dead and alive, real . . . and fake!

The sailors made money by showing their "monsters" to the public, both poor and rich. Regular people paid for a peek. Rich people often bought the monsters or paid for more voyages.

This 1585 map shows monsters in the sea near Iceland. The artist's imagination, fueled by sailors' excited descriptions, painted wild terrors of the sea.

Patrix fiord
Kolevig
Bredevig
Hualo tuo
Rauga sand
Bara
Batrla strang
Vadil
Occidens
C
Krossfiord Gilsfiord
Bald Io...
Pelle strand
Huams suert
Flatey
Bin eyar
Fons cereuisialis,
quando ob do...
quaristi
mutauit
Staphsolt
Breydafiordur
Huams fiord
Hiatus terræ
foetentes
Alfafiord
Ikegur Ʒrand
Hrumfiord
Kolpurfiord
Grinsra fiord
Heigra fell
Lundi
Melaffadur
Gufula vig
Kumbrum vig
Afeyra fnei
Stromfiord
Akranes
Borgarfiord
Hualfiord
Videy
elostes
Tsallaryfiord
Sneuels Iokul
D
Brimnes
Skeryfiord
Ondvertnes
Staps
Stadurfted
Hersey
Beffefted
K
Londranga
Hellar
Haffiorderey
Hafnarfiord
G
Romalanes
Klin vig
E
Keflavig
Grunda vg
Rokianes
Eldey
Foss
communans In
nas enigmas in
albas
F
Geie fuelasker
Geie eiar
Tangi
H

5   10   15   20
Scala milliarium Iflandicorum.

353   354   355   356   357   358   359   360

WHEN LOOKS DECEIVE

Some early explorers brought back strange animals that were mistaken for **mythical** beasts. Other explorers faked the monsters they brought back. They sewed pieces of dead animals together to look like fantastic monsters.

Jenny Hanivers were dead monkey bodies sewn to the tails of large fishes so they looked like mermaids. In the late 1800s, a museum curator hooked together dinosaur backbones and called it a "sea serpent skeleton."

American showman P. T. Barnum's circus was also famous for its so-called "Feegee Mermaids" — similarly faked monster **remains**.

This "Feegee Mermaid" is on display at the Peabody Museum at Harvard University. "Monster mummies" like this still fascinate people.

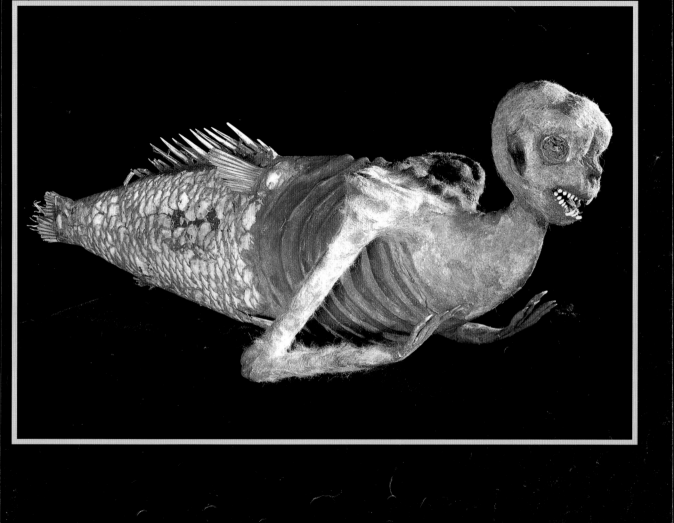

SEA THINGS THAT AREN'T THERE?

Fog and distance sometimes cause a trick of the eye that fools the mind. In such cases, common sea animals might appear to be giant sea serpents or **merpeople**.

Seals, otters, and walruses have heads and eyes the same size and shape as human heads and eyes. They also make noises that sound similar to singing and talking — especially if the listener thinks merpeople speak a different language.

These animals also spend lots of time grooming and playing on rocks. People once thought that merpeople frolicked and fussed with their looks in mirrors for hours.

Giant squid and octopuses, such as this giant Pacific octopus, fed the fears and imaginations of sailors who told wild tales of sea monsters and merpeople.

BIG FISH TALES

Whales, giant squid, moray eels, and fish such as coelacanths or leopardfish still seem a little monstrous to those of us who walk on land. How easy it would be to mistake them for the mythical creatures from that place called "Here Be Monsters!"

After all, the blue whale is the largest animal on Earth. The giant squid has a huge tooth in its mouth and suckers that work as circular knives. A hungry moray eel is just as dangerous as a shark to an unlucky swimmer. And, although coelacanths and leopardfish are harmless, they certainly look big and ugly to us.

From far away, the green moray eel may not look too scary. But, close up, that hungry gleam in its eye and its grim grin may change your mind!

BE THERE MONSTERS?

Are there monsters in the oceans? It depends on what you call a monster. If something as big as a coelacanth can escape notice, what other incredible creatures might be out there?

We may not find anything as fantastic as the Creature from the Black Lagoon. But if we do, we should pay it more respect than the movie scientists did. They tried to improve the Gill Man by removing his gills. As a result, he drowned.

Instead, we should protect any rare and wonderful creatures we find — not help them to death.

The Gill Man, after the operation meant to "help" him be more human: no gills, no scales, no claws. No longer a monster of the deep.

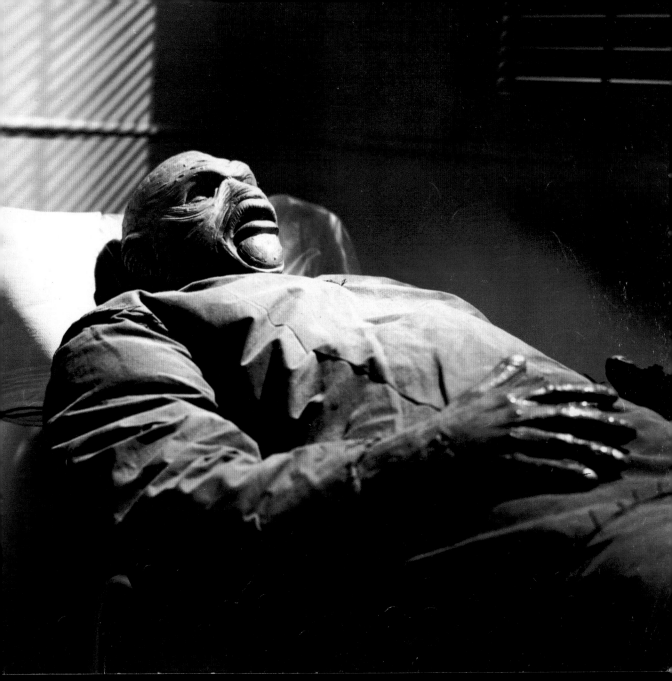

MORE TO READ, VIEW, AND LISTEN TO

Books (Nonfiction)　*A Day in the Life of a Marine Biologist.* David Paige (Troll)
Extremely Weird Sea Creatures. Sarah Lovett (John Muir)
The Leviathans. Tim Dinsdale (Routledge and Kegan Paul)
The Living World. Record Breakers (series). David Lambert
　(Gareth Stevens)
The Loch Ness Monster. Elaine Landau (Millbrook)
Monster Mysteries. Rupert Matthews (Bookwright)
Monsters (series). Janet Perry and Victor Gentle (Gareth Stevens)
Real Live Monsters! Ellen Schecter (Gareth Stevens)
True-Life Monsters of the Prehistoric Seas. Enid Broderick Fisher
　(Gareth Stevens)

Books (Activity)　*Make-up Monsters.* Marcia Lynn Cox (Grosset & Dunlap)
Monsters and Extraterrestrials. Draw, Model, and Paint (series).
　Isidro Sánchez (Gareth Stevens)

Books (Fiction)　*The Boggart and the Monster.* Susan Cooper (Margaret McElderry)
From the Mouth of the Monster Eel. Nancy Bohac Flood (Fulcrum)
Marcie and the Monster of the Bayou. Betty Hager (Zondervan)

Videos (Nonfiction)　*Exploring Marine Biology.* (Human Relations Media)
Finite Oceans. (Discovery Communications)
500 Million Years Beneath the Sea. (Churchill Films)
Food Web. (Disney Educational Productions)
Life Below. (Journal Films)
Why Is This Dolphin Smiling? (Kurtis Productions/WTTW)

Videos (Fiction)　*Creature from the Black Lagoon.* (Universal Studios)
The Creature Walks Among Us. (Universal Studios)
The Magic School Bus Gets Eaten. (Scholastic, Inc./Kid Vision)
20,000 Leagues Under the Sea. (Walt Disney)

Audio　*Songs of the Humpback Whale.* (BMG/Living Music)

WEB SITES

If you have your own computer and Internet access, great! If not, most libraries have Internet access. Go to your library and enter the word *museums* into the library's preferred search engine. See if you can find a museum web page that has exhibits on fossils, mummified mermaids, circus exhibits, deep sea animals, and sea monsters. If any of these museums are close by, you can visit them in person!

The Internet changes every day, and web sites come and go. We believe the sites we recommend here are likely to last, and give the best and most appropriate links for our readers to pursue their interest in sea creatures, real and imaginary.

www.ajkids.com

This is the junior *Ask Jeeves* site – a great research tool.

Some questions to *Ask Jeeves Kids*:
- *Where can I find information about prehistoric sea animals?*
- *What does an African lungfish do when it is out of water?*
- *Where can I find information about fossils of sea life?*

You can also type in words and phrases with a "?" at the end, for example,
- *Coelacanths?*
- *Sea monsters?*

www.mzoo.com

The Miniature Zoo has a special section of monsters and weird critters. Go to the site and click on the Quick Site Index to see pictures and links to many strange and unusual beasties – real and imaginary – from the watery deep!

www.yahooligans.com

This is the junior Yahoo! home page. Click on one of the listed topics (such as Around the World, Science and Nature) for more links. From Around the World, try Anthropology and Archaeology and Mythology and Folklore to find more sites on monsters of the deep. From Science and Nature, you might try Dinosaurs, Animals, Living Things, or Museums and Exhibits to find out more about fossils, sea creatures, and newly discovered animals. You can also search for more information by typing a word in the Yahooligans search engine. Some words to try are: *coelacanth, Galápagos Islands, mermaid.*

www.yucky.com and http://frog.simplenet.com/froggy

Visit these fun sites to find out what it's like to be inside your body and the bodies of other animals. Check out the slimiest, creepiest creatures that live in the water!

GLOSSARY

You can find these words on the pages listed. Reading a word in a sentence helps you understand it even better.

coelacanth (SEE-luh-kanth) — a type of deep-sea fish once thought to have disappeared completely from our oceans 6, 8, 10, 18, 20

extinction (ek-STINK-shun) — the end of existence for a type of animal or plant 6, 8, 10

fossils (FAH-suhlz) — remains of animals or plants that have been preserved inside rock over thousands or millions of years 6, 10

gills — an organ (as in fish) for obtaining oxygen from water 8, 20

ichthyologist (IK-thee-AH-luh-jist) — a scientist who studies fish 10

lungfish — a type of fish that has lungs and can breathe air, like land animals 6, 8

merpeople (MUHR-pea-puhl) — creatures, part human and part fish, believed by many people in the past to live in the oceans of the world 16

mythical (MITH-ih-kuhl) — belonging to stories from the past, but thought (by most people) not to have existed in reality 14, 18

prehistoric (PRE-hiss-TOHR-ick) — coming from a time before history was recorded 6

remains (ree-MAYNZ) — bones, a skeleton, or a dead body 14

INDEX